DRAGONS

& other rare creatures
VOLUME TWO

*Written and Illustrated
by Jessica Cathryn Feinberg*

With special thanks to:

All of my Patreon Subscribers,
fans, friends, and Kickstarter Backers
whose support made this book possible.

My editing & creative support gang:
Janet, Victoria, Gemma, and Daniel!

FIRST EDITION MARCH 2020
Copyright © 2020 Jessica C. Feinberg
All rights reserved.
Paperback ISBN: 978-1-64826-916-5
Hardcover ISBN: 978-1-64826-933-2

Contents

Dear Reader,

In this book I present you with many strange, wondrous, and occasionally dangerous creatures. The information about them has been acquired by many brave persons, mystery seekers, and explorers (names have been withheld for their safety and privacy).

I have endeavored to compile and present as many of these marvelous beasts as I can in this volume, and hopefully many more magical books to follow.

Readers are encouraged to approach this book with a sense of wonder, an open mind, and, of course, caution where necessary as some of the creatures are deadly.

Enjoy the creatures!

CREATURE TYPES

<u>Dragon</u> is the common all-encompassing name for creatures with the *draco* gene.

<u>Western Dragons</u> are most common in the United States, Canada, and Europe. They have reptilian features and anywhere from 2-4 limbs. They may or may not have wings.

<u>Drakes</u> are a subset of western dragons that tend to be on the smaller side and either have no wings, or their wings are small. They always have at least two limbs, but may have more.

<u>Eastern Dragons</u>, also called Lungs, are from Asia and usually have more dog and mammal-like features including fur or whiskers. They are long with sinuous, serpent-like bodies, blunter snouts, and may have both fur and scale. Eastern Dragons may or may not have limbs, but they never have wings.

<u>Wyrms</u> are dragons without limbs or wings. They are sometimes also referred to as serpents.

<u>Wyverns</u> are winged dragons that never have more than two limbs, and many do not have any limbs at all. They are also referred to as flying serpents or winged serpents.

<u>Coatls</u> are wyverns with feathers and are usually from Central America.

<u>Hydras</u> are dragons with multiple heads. Most Hydra species may grow additional heads over time, but this is species specific.

<u>Insectoid</u> creatures are those with insect-like features such as extra jointed limbs, and wings that resemble butterflies or dragonflies.

Amphibious creatures are those that can live in water and also on land.

Aquatic creatures are those that dwell in water and generally have some fish-like features (like fins).

Metal is a creature classification used for one or more of the following reasons:
1. The creature physically resembles a specific metal.
2. The creature is affiliated with one or more metals.
3. The creature is a living metal creature.

Clockwork creatures are a subset of metal creatures that are made of metal and gears. They may be simply a machine, brought to life by magic, or inhabited by a dragon spirit.

Hybrids are creatures that are mixtures of several different animals or other creatures. Hybrids mixed with humans are also referred to as ___ folk such as Merfolk, Fishfolk, Birdfolk and so forth.

Faeries or **Fae** refer to a variety of creatures including small flying fairies, gnomes, dwarves, trolls, giants etc. The smaller species of these like gnomes, brownies, and dwarves are also called the Little People.

Gorgons are hybrids of humans and snakes or dragons.

Avians are creatures that are part bird or bird-like.

Felines are creatures that are part cat.

Ethereal creatures are those without physically tangible bodies, including spirits and ghosts.

Strange & Mischievous

Let us begin this book with a section containing some of the most strange and dangerous creatures!

Here are bizarre hybrids, mischievous dragons, and creepy critters.

Many of these creatures are deadly and have no qualms when it comes to killing animals, other creatures, and even humans. One should not attempt to seek out these species without an expert guide and proper protection.

Western Black Cave Dragon

Occidentis malum antrum draco

This rare species of black dragon is quite large and only found in Central and Northern Europe. Most who encounter Black Cave Dragons do not survive, but the few who have returned describe a creature over forty feet long with powerful acidic breath. In the middle ages this dragon species was often one that knights sought to best in battle or that villages paid tributes to in order to protect their livestock.

In modern times Black Cave Dragons rarely leave the deep cave systems they call home, choosing to avoid the surface and feed on underground creatures only. Black Cave Dragons are famous treasure hoarders, but it is a suicide mission to attempt to take even one coin of their hoard. Their hearing is so acute that they can track even the softest clink of coin out of place.

Bad-Luck Lung

Mala fortuna draco

This Asian dragon can live up to a thousand years and is very cunning. While many luck lungs bring those who encounter them good fortune, this one brings only bad luck and seems to enjoy causing it. Some even think it feeds off the energy of those it curses.

Bad Luck Lungs dwell in deep mountain caves throughout Asia. Those who have the misfortune to find one experience terrible luck for months after, sometimes so severely that it results in their death.

It is recommended that Dragon Watchers should avoid this species whenever possible. Should you be cursed by a Bad-Luck Lung, seek the help of an experienced gypsy or bruja.

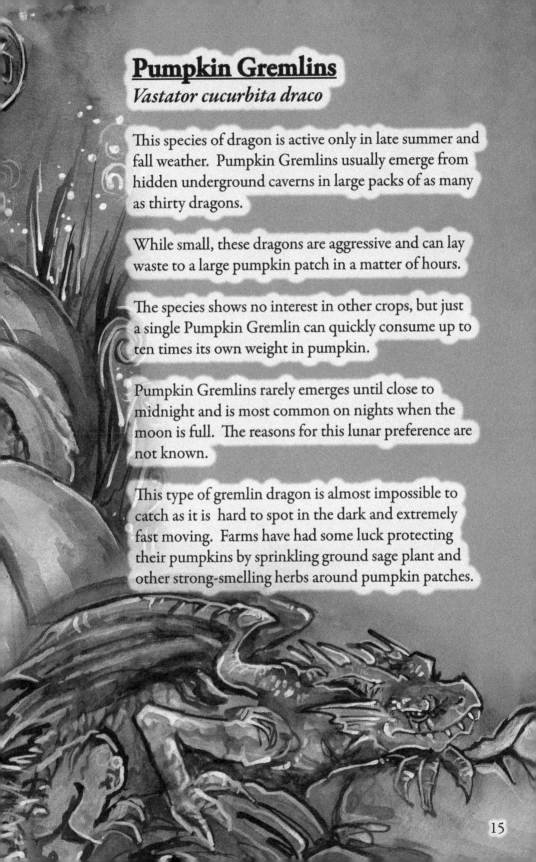

Pumpkin Gremlins
Vastator cucurbita draco

This species of dragon is active only in late summer and fall weather. Pumpkin Gremlins usually emerge from hidden underground caverns in large packs of as many as thirty dragons.

While small, these dragons are aggressive and can lay waste to a large pumpkin patch in a matter of hours.

The species shows no interest in other crops, but just a single Pumpkin Gremlin can quickly consume up to ten times its own weight in pumpkin.

Pumpkin Gremlins rarely emerges until close to midnight and is most common on nights when the moon is full. The reasons for this lunar preference are not known.

This type of gremlin dragon is almost impossible to catch as it is hard to spot in the dark and extremely fast moving. Farms have had some luck protecting their pumpkins by sprinkling ground sage plant and other strong-smelling herbs around pumpkin patches.

Banshee Drake

Clamatis mortis draco

Named for its likeness in sound to the Irish Banshee spirit, the Banshee Drake is known for loud, haunting cries that pierce the night. As with the more traditional Banshee, hearing the Banshee Drake is said to mean that someone you care about has died or is about to die.

Banshee Drakes are more often heard than seen. The few who have seen them (and lived to tell the tale) describe a horrible undead dragon around three feet long with sharp teeth and grasping claws. As a specimen has yet to be captured for study, it is not clear if the Banshee Drake is some sort of ethereal spirit or a more solid species of dragon.

Patchwork Dragon

This dragon is not a specific species, but rather a macabre combination of many species. These undead creatures are usually created with necrotic magic for a specific purpose. The species of dragons chosen to use for parts are usually related to the task the dragon is meant for.

Once the dragon has fulfilled this purpose the magic dissipates and the Patchwork Dragon falls to bits. This type of magic is rarely used and generally frowned upon (and even illegal in some countries) as the dragons the parts are harvested from are not always dead first.

Dragon Henge

This ancient stone circle is used by dragon species of all shapes and sizes as a meeting place. Dragon Henge is said to be somewhere in England or Ireland. A few old photos of the circle exist, but today those who seek it out always get lost along the way. This suggests some sort of magic protecting the circle from humans.

The purpose of the dragon gatherings remains a mystery. Some researchers think these are meetings between dragon species to maintain peace or make choices about how to deal with humans. Others insist the dragons are doing some sort of magical ritual to help maintain balance in the universe.

Great Dragon Trees

The Great Dragon Trees are a handful of large, old trees that seem to draw dragons to them. Why the dragons give special attention to, and group at these trees is not known.

Several teams of Dragon Watchers are currently conducting an observational study of such trees in Europe, Africa, and Asia. They are tracking the variety of species, number of dragons, time spent in the tree, and any notable or abnormal behavior.

As many as a dozen different species have been reported in the branches of one such tree at a time. They sleep, play, and forage for food.

Interestingly, the dragons never show any aggression towards each other, even if a larger species would normally prey on a smaller one. It's as if these trees are some sort of peaceful neutral territory or perhaps of some spiritual significance to dragon species.

Ley line patterns around the trees and other potentially magical elements are also being considered and compared.

IODS is working on a preservation program to ensure such trees will be protected, at least until further data about their significance both to dragons and the environment as a whole is determined.

Very-Deadly Hedgehog
Ipsum mortiferum erinaceus

Found only in Asia and Africa, this hedgehog species is on the smaller side with full grown specimens at just under six inches. Their small size is well compensated for with sharper spines, faster movement, and a highly aggressive attitude. Very-Deadly Hedgehogs can band together into groups of two or three and take down much larger animals. Their prey even includes humans and dragons!

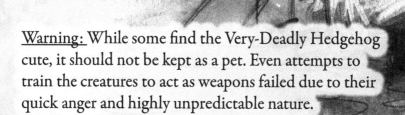

<u>Warning:</u> While some find the Very-Deadly Hedgehog cute, it should not be kept as a pet. Even attempts to train the creatures to act as weapons failed due to their quick anger and highly unpredictable nature.

Anthrotaur

Minotaurus e converso

This European species is a hybrid of human and bull, much like its better known Minotaur cousin, but with reversed parts. While very strong, the Anthrotaur is a gentle species which likes to be left alone to nap in fields of wildflowers.

Sadly, they were considered abominations by the Ancient Greeks. Many were killed by soldiers and farmers. The remaining population sticks to secluded high mountain meadows. Only the most patient and gentle of observers can spot them.

A fairly famous Anthrotaur was apart of a 1930s traveling sideshow of hybrids in where he was known as "Bull-Head Bobbert".

African Lopeajack

Lepus Cornutus contrarium

Rodrick Smitherson III discovered the Lopeajack while on Safari in the 1940s and named it after a similar creature he'd heard of in the American Southwest. Where the better-known Jackalope hybrid is a rabbit with a little antelope, the Lopeajack is mainly antelope with just a touch of rabbit. Native to African Savannah Grasslands this species can run-hop at great speed. Herds of Lopeajacks are less common today, but still occasionally reported.

Turquoise Goblin Queen
Arabian Goblin Species

The Turquoise Goblin Queen is thought to be a species of Goblin from Arabia, but has proved highly elusive, making further study difficult.

Legends of the Turquoise Goblin Queen tell of her palace filled with the finest of turquoise stones. This massive underground structure is guarded by many goblins and strange goblin-toad hybrid creatures.

These rocky-toad creatures were depicted in old journals as being both defenders of the queen and steeds ridden by her most trusted soldiers.

Monstrous Butterfly Skitter

Papilionem monstrum

This Japanese species of skitter monster has led to many terrifying tales. The stories say it is a huge cave-dwelling creature that eats humans after torturing them for fun.

The truth is that the Butterfly Skitter is only a foot or so in height and very timid. Like butterflies it loves nectar, but it isn't very graceful and tends to chomp down entire flowers. It avoids humans, skittering away while uttering tiny screams.

If cornered it will fly into the faces of those attacking and even bite them with tiny sharp teeth, but this rarely proves fatal. Butterfly Skitters usually hide away in the foothills of remote Japanese mountains, hoping to avoid contact with larger species that might wish it harm.

Vampire Sloth
Sanguinem bibens bradypodidae

Vampire Sloth sightings have been traced back to the 1500s in journals and letters. Experts now think that the species is actually much older. They theorize that a mutation caused this evolutionary offshoot as far as 15 to 20 million years ago.

On the edge of extinction, the Vampire Sloth has only been spotted a handful of times in South America over the last thirty years. The species is active only at night, and even then it is sitting still or very slow-moving, making it difficult to see.

With large fangs and deep-set yellow eyes, it is easily differentiated from other sloth species. When ready to strike the Vampire Sloth will drop suddenly onto its prey and swiftly incapacitate them. Then the Vampire Sloth spends many long hours slowly draining the blood from its victim. They have been known to attack humans who venture into their territory.

Stories say some famous humanoid vampires may have kept these creatures as minions or pets.

Wendigo
Also called Weendigo, Windego, Wiindgoo, Windgo, and Windigoag (plural)

These fearsome creatures were first reported by Algonquian tribes in Canada. There are several species variations which have lead to mixed descriptions and lore that is only tricky to sort out.

All species of Wendigo are extremely dangerous as they crave meat and will specifically seek out humans as a food source. Some stories say they evolved from cannibalistic humans, and others say that they started as evil spirits who possessed the bodies of evil men.

Some Wendigo species are more human in appearance, while others have more deer-like features with antlers. Lore states that a Wendigo grows larger and more animal-like in relation to the number of humans and animals they have consumed.

Recently there have been reports of at least one young or baby Wendigo (as shown in the artist's rendition at the right), but if that is due to reproduction or to something that possessed the body of a human child it is unclear. Most active in the coldest winter months.

Fae Creatures

Fae species come from a place known as *Faerie* which is theorized to overlap with our world, possibly in some sort of parallel dimension.

Bridges or gateways between our world and Faerie were once common and the creatures from Faerie often visited our world bringing magic and mystery with them.

Over time the connection between worlds faded. Today, the remaining gateways are kept secret and closely guarded.

Many fae including gnomes, elves, dwarves, and trolls remain in our world as the descendents of those long-ago visitors.

Faerie dragons were thought extinct until recently. The first new sightings were in the early 2000s and several dozen species have been identified since then.

Perhaps these creatures are hatching from long dormant eggs, or they have been hidden for hundreds of years for some unknown reason, but are now revealing themselves.

A few whispers among dragon scholars suggest that a new gateway has been opened or even that these creatures are intentionally being brought through such a portal. But who is bringing them and why remains a mystery.

Silver Leaf Wyvern
Foliis argenteis fae draco

This enchanting shimmering dragon appears silver, blue, or pink depending upon the lighting. To date, it has only been reported on nights with fairly bright moonlight. Four and a half inches long, the Silver Leaf Wyvern moves with swift, short, flits of speed. Those who spot it seem unable to look away until it is gone.

Sapphire Fae Dragon
Sapphirus fae draco

A extremely rare Faerie Dragon species, there are only a few
documented sightings of this dragon in the last twenty years.
At only five inches in length, this flower-hungry creature is
dainty and swift, making it harder to spot. It can be lured out
of hiding with colorful flowers, sea glass, or gemstones which
it will snatch up and hoard in a secret den.

<u>Red Fae Wyvern</u>
Rubrum fae draco

A small faerie dragon, the Red Fae Wyvern loves to soak up sunshine in meadows of wildflowers. It both encourages flowers to grow and greatly relishes snapping off their blooms and chomping them down. Rarely dangerous to humans, but can bite painfully and should not be handled without thick gloves.

Stained Glasswing Drake
Picta alae specularibus fae draco

Glasswings are a grouping of fae creatures with wings that resemble cut or stained glass. The Stained Glasswing Drake is a tiny jewel-like dragon only two inches in size. While the species is becoming more common in domestic gardens, they are rarely noticed unless the sun catches their wings. This drake eats small insects and brings good health to plants that were previously ailing in the area.

Lesser Tufted Fae Drake

Plumulae fae draco minor

This two and a half inch drake has iridescent scales and feather-like tufts. A recent discovery, not much is known about this species except that they are proficient with lesser glamour magics.

Pastel Glasswing Drake
Pastel alae specularibus fae draco

This beautiful glasswing grows up to six inches and is considered a form of luck dragon. Over the last ten years they have become more common as they are being bred for use by witches and sorcerers who specialize in luck magics. The Pastel Glasswing only has a 2 to 2.5 year lifespan, though they are thought to live longer in Faerie and just don't fair as well in our world.

<u>**Greater Tufted Fae Drake**</u>
Plumulae fae draco major

The larger species of Tufted Fae Drake is around four feet tall
with brightly colored scales and feather-like tufts. These tufts
may shift in color if the creature is excited or alarmed. Found
mainly in tropical climates. Requires warm temperatures to
survive and greatly enjoys fruit from both our world and faerie.

Orb Guardian
Orbis custos fae draco

Small, rare dragons with dragon-fly like wings, the Orb Guardians watch over faerie and dragon orbs. They take this task seriously and protect their orb from any who would use its magic for harm. While not physically formidable, the species is highly proficient in faerie magic and will simply transform attackers into small insects, then eat them.

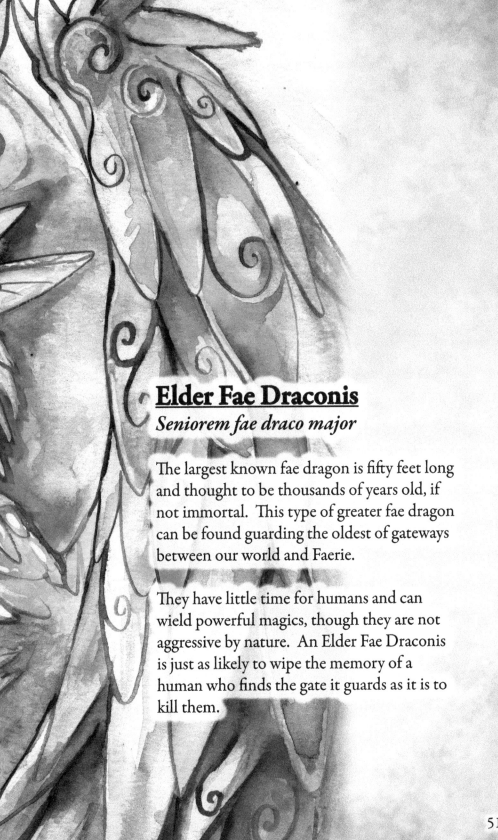

Elder Fae Draconis
Seniorem fae draco major

The largest known fae dragon is fifty feet long and thought to be thousands of years old, if not immortal. This type of greater fae dragon can be found guarding the oldest of gateways between our world and Faerie.

They have little time for humans and can wield powerful magics, though they are not aggressive by nature. An Elder Fae Draconis is just as likely to wipe the memory of a human who finds the gate it guards as it is to kill them.

Fae Drakaina
Femina draco fae

Around a hundred years ago some Drakania found their way through a faerie gate. This resulted in the crossbreeding of elves and other fae with the dragon-human hybrids. Thus several Fae Drakaina hybrid variations were born.

Fae Drakaina vary in appearance, but always have more pronounced horns and very strong magical powers as compared to the original Drakaina species.

A group of these creatures started their own dragon-fae sorceress guild which is much feared and avoided by the lesser fae species.

This species is not known to venture into the human realm often and generally regards itself as superior to the Drakaina species that they evolved from.

Butterfly Masked Sprite
Papilio ratissimae imaginis fae

A foot-high delicate sprite, this species was first named for the butterfly-like masks they appear to wear. With further observation, the British Society for the Preservation of Lesser Fae (BSPLF) discovered that these are actually wing-like growths on the face.

The purpose of these growths is theorized to be related to magic, as they flutter when the sprite is using magic. Magical abilities documented for the species include minor magical plant charms and small glamours.

Glamour Magic

"Glamour" refers to a specific form of magic which makes people or things appear as other than they actually are.

The most commonly documented glamours are very subtle, often barely changing the appearance of what they are cast on. Yet they greatly alter how people interact with the glamoured person or object - it may be irresistibly attractive or completely fade into the background and be ignored.

Greater glamours that completely alter appearance are rarer, at least in our world, though some think there are many fae among us who are simply glamoured to go unnoticed.

Faerie Courts

It has long been told that the fae are divided into two groups: the Seelie Court and the Unseelie Court. Those that are generally well-meaning or "good" belong to the Seelie Court and those that are darker, malicious, or "evil" are in the Unseelie Court.

We now know that there are many more groupings or courts of fae, perhaps separate from the Seelie and Unseelie, or maybe as sub-groups within them. The information on this is often conflicting and muddled, suggesting that they are in a state of regular flux or that the fae just want to mislead those who would learn about them.

Greater Shadow Fae
Nympharum umbrae major

The Greater Shadow Fae are members of the Unseelie Court dating back hundreds of years. They are rarely spotted by humans, and those who do spot them often doubt what they saw and assume it was just a shadow. While they are said to wield great magical power, this type of fae is more often in the background, busy pulling the strings that cause faerie or human events to occur while they go unnoticed. They should be avoided and never trusted or trifled with.

Solar & Lunar Dryads
Solis/ Lunares dryadesque

Dryads are a fae species of tree spirit or nymph. They usually cannot stray far from the trees they are connected to and the oldest dryads have become part of the tree itself.

Lunar and Solar Dryad species are rare to spot outside of Faerie. They reside in the most ancient of trees and only appear under strong sun or moonlight.

Both species of dryad occasionally make their homes in the same groups of trees but never appear at the same time except in the rare case of a lunar or solar eclipse.

Fall Dryad
Autumnales Dryadesque

Fall Dryads or "Autumn Maids" are a fae species from the Seelie Court that only appears in the fall season. It is believed that they hibernate near or within large groups of trees and only emerge when the leaves of the trees begin to change color and drop.

This type of dryad is usually found near groves of maple or oak trees. On the Autumn Equinox they are sometimes spotted in small groups dancing around the trees in a swirl of leaves and moonlight.

As with most fae species, one should never take food from dryads, make bargains with them, or join in their celebrations. Humans who have attempted to do so have gone missing for months or even years. Returning, they claim that only a single night has passed.

Book Gnomes
Librum gnomus

Knowledge of these little people comes mainly from the journals of Jason Creekworth circa 1972. There is just enough corroborating evidence from other encounters to confirm they are a real species and not a figment of Creekworth's imagination.

Creekworth's journals tell of becoming lost deep in the New Forest in Southern England. After wandering some time the air around him seemed to change and the sky became a strange shifting color. He then stumbled upon a large city that appeared made of books in all shapes, colors, and sizes.

RARE BOOKS

HERE THERE
BE BOOKS

63

The inhabitants of this "book city" were around three feet tall and, from comparing similar descriptions, seem to be some type of gnome.

Creekworth refers to these beings as the People of the Books, but today they are more commonly called Book Gnomes.

While no other individual has been able to describe such a city, Book Gnomes are sometimes spotted in libraries or large private book collections "borrowing" books.

They appear to value the written word above most other things and are only aggressive towards those who abuse or damage books.

This species dresses with traditional tall, brightly colored gnome caps. They are often accompanied by small dragons, rabbits, or other animals. These animals seem to be more of a companion than a pet and may assist the Book Gnome in a multitude of ways.

It is also worth noting that Creekworth mentions the books these gnomes collect cover a variety of languages from human to dragon to fae to ancient scripts. Perhaps this makes them the most proficient linguists in existence today.

Tomte

Also known as Nisse or Tonttu

This variety of gnome is found only in Nordic countries and is most common in Finland, Norway, and Sweden.

Tomte are usually seen in December, when they don bright colors to celebrate the winter solstice. The common variety are only a few inches high, but there is also a rare three foot high Tomte species.

Most often spotted are the elder males, with long white beards and colorful pointed caps. The Tomte traditions assign these men to hunting, foraging, and borrowing (from humans). Children and female Tomte stay in hidden villages performing tasks like cooking, building, weaving, and so forth.

Tomte have been around for so long that countless traditions and superstitions have formed around them. The most notable of these is that gifts of food, such as porridge or cookies, must be left in tribute on Yule or Christmas night.

Those who ignore this tradition will become the victims of nasty pranks. Farmers might find the tails of all their cows tied in knots, buckets may be overturned, and precious heirlooms missing or broken.

More recent stories describe Tomte accompanied by goats spotted on Christmas Eve. They will leave gifts on the doorsteps of those they feel are most deserving.

Tomte possess immense strength, and can carry ten times their own body weight!

Tomte and other cold-dwelling gnome species usually have
small villages or clusters of homes in which to shelter from
the winter weather and the prying eyes of humans.

Some are well-hidden in the trunks of trees, deep in the
forest. Others may be carved into rocky outcrops, small
caves, or burrowed into the sides of hills.

Gnomes living close to humans may use discarded flower
pots, cans, and even shoes in the construction of their homes.

Legendary Arctic Dwarves

The well-known dwarf species choose to carve their homes, halls, cities, and castles in mountain depths. Yet there are a few cold-dwelling species who choose, instead, to carve structures from ice.

Only a little is known about Arctic Dwarves, as the last reported sighting was well over a hundred years ago. A journal and old blurry photograph from the late 1800s document a large settlement somewhere in Norway or Iceland. The illustration shown here is based on that photograph.

The journal tells of two foot high Frost Dwarves and slightly larger Ice Dwarves living together in great halls and towers, entirely made of ice.

The photograph shows a shape thought to be a dragon atop this ice city, but it isn't clear enough to tell if this is a decorative carving or an actual living dragon (perhaps guarding the city).

A number of expeditions from the Institute of Obscure Draconian Studies have attempted to locate the ice city and determine if dragons are present there, but so far none have had success.

It is worth noting that the 1938 Swalberg expedition went missing after their first week of exploration. Stories say those ten brave dragon watchers found the city and, for some reason, stayed there. Yet other stories have a more grim outcome, with Ice Dragons and even Ice Dwarves, butchering the expedition.

Dwarven Dragon Riders

Dwarves generally dwell in or near mountains and hills, mine them for precious metals or gems, and forge what they mine into sought after items ranging from swords to decorative adornments. Dwarves are also known to be great warriors, wielding large axes or swords with mighty strength.

Yet there are many types of dwarves that are lesser known including the dwarven dragon riders. This small grouping of dwarves is willing to leave the ground and take to the sky on the backs of red wyverns. Special saddles and harnesses are used for this purpose, scaled to their shorter statures. Dragon riders are not usually trained for battle in the air and are mainly used for reconnaissance or to carry long distance messages.

GORGONS

The Gorgon is a hybrid creature that combines snake and human DNA. Most Gorgons are female in appearance (except for a rumored Gorgoman species, but it is thought to be a hoax).

The best known of Gorgons is Medusa, from greek tales of creatures and gods. This species is considered a *traditional* Gorgon, but there are many other variations that have been reported worldwide. In fact, Gorgon species are so widespread that experts now think they must have evolved or been created independently, rather than splitting off from one parent species.

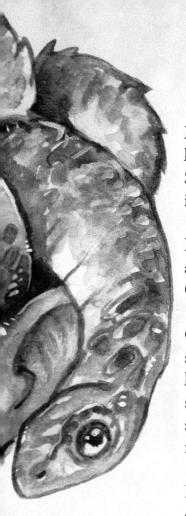

Most Gorgons have the ability to petrify humans or other threats in some way. Stone is the most common (but wood and ice have also occurred).

It is worth noting that this is a defensive ability, not one used to hunt as most Gorgons cannot ingest rock!

Gorgon babies are fairly rare and we are still compiling data about them. It is known that they hatch from eggs like snakes and most species shed their skin several times during the growth process from child to adult.

Baby Gorgons develop their powers at different ages depending on species. The most traditional species seem to get theirs as a toddler. This makes them particularly dangerous as their tantrums can turn nearby creatures to stone.

A few of the more rare Gorgon species such as the Ice Gorgon do not develop a freezing gaze until they reach puberty.

Egyptian Gorgon
Naja haje femina

The Egyptian Gorgon was both feared and revered by the Ancient Egyptians who thought her to be an embodiment of the cobra-headed goddess *Meretsege* (now suspected to be another hybrid species that has gone extinct). There have not been any sightings of the species in the last thousand years, but many think they simply retreated underground and kill any who find them.

Fungal Gorgon
Fungos serpens femina

This species is adaptable to both temperate and tropical regions of the world. The brown-green coloration of the Fungal Gorgon and ability to move both swiftly and silently makes them experts at remaining hidden from those who would seek them out. The fungal growths upon their bodies are something of a mystery and said to have strange magical properties if ingested.

Siren Gorgon
Sirene serpens femina

A creature both incredibly rare and beautiful, the Siren Gorgon causes paralysis with her song, rather than her gaze. The disappearance of many travelers in the Mediterranean is blamed on this species. Since only a few have lived to tell of the creature, it is unclear how common encounters with one are.

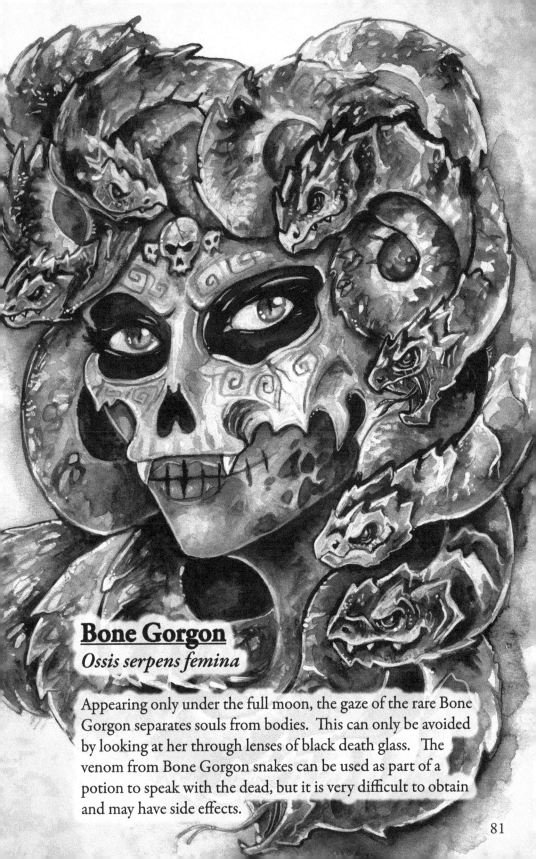

Bone Gorgon
Ossis serpens femina

Appearing only under the full moon, the gaze of the rare Bone Gorgon separates souls from bodies. This can only be avoided by looking at her through lenses of black death glass. The venom from Bone Gorgon snakes can be used as part of a potion to speak with the dead, but it is very difficult to obtain and may have side effects.

Ice Gorgon
Glacies serpens femina

Very rare and only ever reported in deep Icelandic Ice Caves, this
species of Gorgon blends in perfectly with her surroundings.
Those who do spot an Ice Gorgon usually do so too late, as
her gaze can freeze humans solid in under sixty seconds. Like
Gorgon Queens, the Ice Gorgon has dragons rather than snakes
growing upon her head. Each ice dragon is able to breathe
deadly blasts of frost, making the species even more dangerous.

Inferno Gorgon

Ignis serpens femina

This is the rarest reported Gorgon species to date, though it is not entirely clear if that is due to how few Inferno Gorgons there are or simply that those who encounter them do not survive their flames.

Clockwork Gorgon

This clockwork-human hybrid was rumored to have been constructed during the Second Great Clockwork War as a form of scout. The snake heads were able to somehow take in and transmit the surroundings of the creature back to a home base. This information is based on a few partial blue prints and stories from veteran soldiers in the war. No other evidence has been found of these creatures to date.

Cyber Gorgon

Even stranger than the Clockwork Gorgon is a creature dubbed the "Cyber Gorgon". Little is known about this hybrid creature and the technology involved in creating her. She is said to have been destroyed in a factory explosion in the 1980s. Some blurry photos from that time and an old audio journal are the only surviving evidence of her existence. A few think she was a time traveler from the future, but others find this theory too fanciful.

Snakania

Contrarium serpens femina

A species of snake-folk this creature is known as an Inverse Gorgon because its serpent-like face is surrounded by growths with human-like faces.

The Snakania has a main head and torso that is serpent-like, but also has four arms and the legs of a human female.

While able to speak, the species chooses not to interact with most humans. Snakania are fierce warriors. While they do not have any abilities with their gaze, they are almost unmatched in sword combat. Snakania dwell in well-hidden cave villages in the middle-east.

Mechanical Marvels

Clockwork dinosaurs and cybernetic dragons are just a few of the unique mechanical creatures collected in this portion of the book for your perusal.

While a few are considered "species", most are singular creations or only exist in a small number. Where sketches and photo reference were available they were used, otherwise the renderings of these creatures are based on written descriptions and the artist's imagination.

Sparrow Time-Keepers

These four inch clockwork birds were hand crafted by Austrian clock-workers in the early 1900s. Their delicate mechanics made them both expensive and sought-after by wealthy collectors.

They functioned as time keepers in a number of different ways. Made to sound an alarm at a specific time, count down an amount of time, or simply chirp the hour much like a clock chime.

Clockwork Sparrows were sometimes sold in sets with different time-keeping purposes and elaborate trees or cages where they perched. Due to their fragile nature few remain in working order today.

Clockwork Piranha

During the Second Great Clockwork War many small mechanical submersibles were used to spy on North Atlantic island bases. A few clockwork war submarines were also said to be a part of the war, but no blueprints or remains of these have been found. The Clockwork Piranha was developed as a countermeasure against these enemy watercraft.

Only a foot long, these small magic-powered fish were deployed in schools to destroy water-based threats. A rare mysterious mineral was used for their teeth which enabled them to easily bite through the hulls of any craft they encountered. Some think a few schools of these creatures are still around in the vicinity of Bermuda.

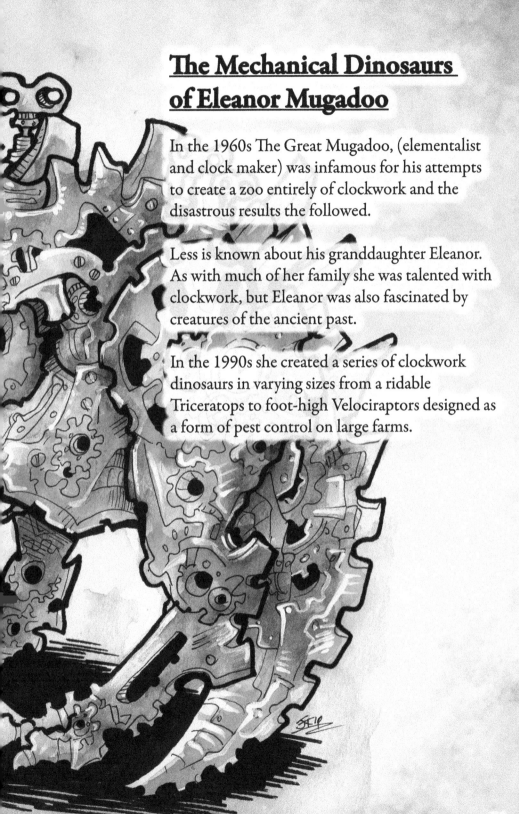

The Mechanical Dinosaurs of Eleanor Mugadoo

In the 1960s The Great Mugadoo, (elementalist and clock maker) was infamous for his attempts to create a zoo entirely of clockwork and the disastrous results the followed.

Less is known about his granddaughter Eleanor. As with much of her family she was talented with clockwork, but Eleanor was also fascinated by creatures of the ancient past.

In the 1990s she created a series of clockwork dinosaurs in varying sizes from a ridable Triceratops to foot-high Velociraptors designed as a form of pest control on large farms.

Over time the creations of Eleanor became less common in the clockwork community and she became more and more secretive about her work.

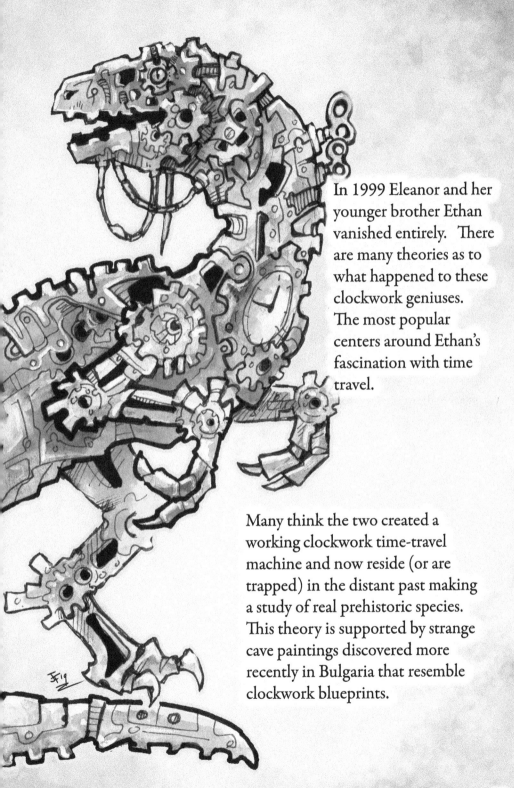

In 1999 Eleanor and her younger brother Ethan vanished entirely. There are many theories as to what happened to these clockwork geniuses. The most popular centers around Ethan's fascination with time travel.

Many think the two created a working clockwork time-travel machine and now reside (or are trapped) in the distant past making a study of real prehistoric species. This theory is supported by strange cave paintings discovered more recently in Bulgaria that resemble clockwork blueprints.

The Legendary Gear Sphinx

The Gear Sphinx is a giant twenty foot tall magically-powered creature said to guard the lost clockwork city of Angra Sha Rhirki somewhere in the mountains of Sri Lanka. The creature is mentioned in the journals of a number of explorers from the 1600-1800s as well as legends passed down verbally by storytellers.

Like all Sphinxes the Gear Sphinx is an expert when it comes to riddles and puzzles. Her clockwork body fits into the workings of the gates guarding the city making her physically required for entry.

Stories say she will only open the gates for those who answer three riddles correctly. What these questions are and their answers has been lost to time. This Sphinx is said to be the only creature of her kind. Most who seek her and the city she guards never return.

The Mechanized Bicorn

This non-functioning beast currently resides in the Grand Clockwork Library. The creature was most definitely intended to resemble a Bicorn (two horned panther-cow hybrid), but whatever inhabited or powered the creature has been inactive for many years.

About twelve feet tall, the Mechanized Bicorn can be found in a large display case in the northwest corner of Hall G. While a few enthusiasts have tried to restore function and power to the beast over the years, thus far none have succeeded.

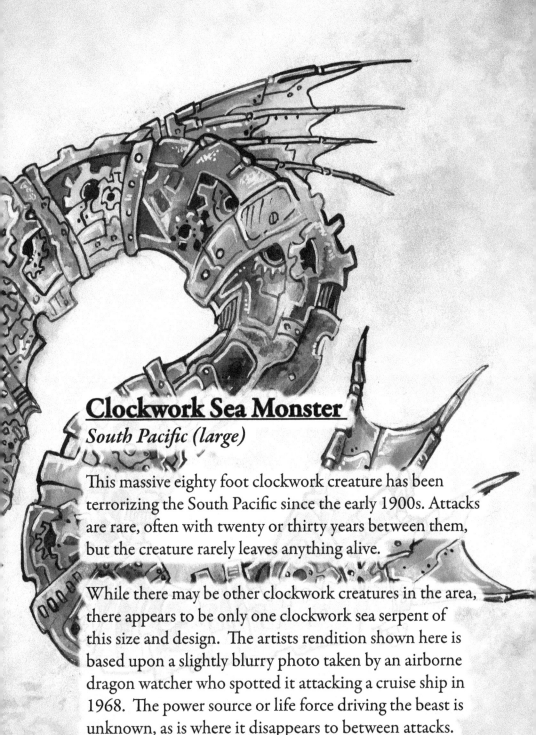

Clockwork Sea Monster
South Pacific (large)

This massive eighty foot clockwork creature has been terrorizing the South Pacific since the early 1900s. Attacks are rare, often with twenty or thirty years between them, but the creature rarely leaves anything alive.

While there may be other clockwork creatures in the area, there appears to be only one clockwork sea serpent of this size and design. The artists rendition shown here is based upon a slightly blurry photo taken by an airborne dragon watcher who spotted it attacking a cruise ship in 1968. The power source or life force driving the beast is unknown, as is where it disappears to between attacks.

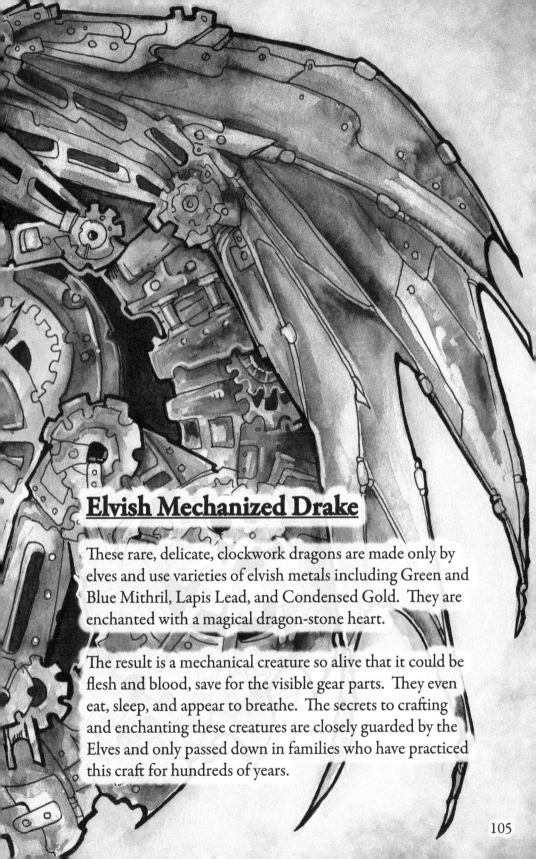

Elvish Mechanized Drake

These rare, delicate, clockwork dragons are made only by elves and use varieties of elvish metals including Green and Blue Mithril, Lapis Lead, and Condensed Gold. They are enchanted with a magical dragon-stone heart.

The result is a mechanical creature so alive that it could be flesh and blood, save for the visible gear parts. They even eat, sleep, and appear to breathe. The secrets to crafting and enchanting these creatures are closely guarded by the Elves and only passed down in families who have practiced this craft for hundreds of years.

Cybernetic Dragon Rider

In the early 1980s there was a series of assassination attempts on members of the secretive Cyberchanters Guild. Little is known about this group other than that they were doing dangerous experiments combining magic and cybernetics. All but one of these attempts was foiled by a mysterious dragon rider.

Grainy footage from several locations shows her and her dragon to be at least partly mechanical. Even today, this technology is still light years ahead of ours. Soon after her appearance the Cyberchanters seemed to vanish, perhaps disbanded, dead, or in even deeper hiding.

There are many conspiracy theories surrounding both the Cyberchanters and the mysterious Cybernetic Dragon Rider. Some say she came from the future to change or preserve certain events, others say she came from a distant planet or hidden civilization with highly advanced technology.

MYTHIC FELINES

The study of feline creature species as a focus is fairly recent, started only in the late 1990s by a woman called Brygid Murphy. Her interest began with the Irish Cat Sidhe, but quickly spread to other parts of the world and mythology.

Previously, mythic cats and feline cryptids were not studied collectively and rarely compared to each other. Those who specialize in Felythic Studies have discovered new species and furthered our understanding on the nature of all mythic cats.

Horned Black Bat Cat
Vespertilio felis draco

This species is often confused with the Bat Winged Cat (*volans vespertilionem felis*), but the Horned Black Bat Cat is, in fact, not a bat hybrid at all! The creature was proclaimed a Bat Cat by those who first documented it in the mid 1800s. Superstitious minded folks even claimed these cats were a type of demon.

The true origin of this species wasn't uncovered until the 1990s when detailed DNA tests were performed. We now know this species is a hybrid of Black Dragon and Domestic Black Cat. The dragon DNA is responsible for the bat-like wings as well as the horns.

The length and number of horns vary from two to six and develop in the first year of the Bat Cat's life. This species is always black with pink, red, or dark blue wings.

This feline-dragon makes an excellent familiar or family pet. Training is most successful if the Bat Cat is introduced to their humans at a bat-kitten (also called a Bitten).

111

Tabby Bat Cat
Volans vespertilionem felis

Felines with feather or bat wings have been documented as far back as the stone age where they appeared in paintings and carvings. The number of domestic bat-winged cats was greatly reduced in the middle ages as Christianity spread across Europe and anything with bat wings was associated with the Devil and killed.

The Tabby Bat Cat was one of the first to bounce back in numbers. Today they are often kept as a familiar or companion to kitchen witches. Stories say they bring good luck in the kitchen and imbue anything baked there with random magical properties.

A few Cabbit species have been reported in North America, including some sort of Cabbit-Jackalope mix dubbed the *Cabalope*. Some say this creature is a hoax as only a handful of people claim to have seen it.

Cabbit
Lepus cattus

The Cabbit is a hybrid of domestic cat and some type of rabbit, probably a long eared hare species. A number of Cabbit variations exist, the best known is found in Japan where it has inspired a number of book and film characters. A Scottish Cabbit species has been documented more recently and can be differentiated by its short nubby tail and resemblance to a Manx cat.

The Japanese Cabbit is usually seen as a trouble maker, perhaps part faerie in origin. Occasionally they have been loyal companions or come to those in need, but more often they have fun creating chaos with their mischief.

Egyptian Winged Cat

Aegyptia volantes cattus

This four foot cat species is thought to be the inspiration for the Ancient Egyptians worship of the goddess Bast (warrior and protector of felines). Due to black market pet trade and poor treatment, Egyptian Winged Cats are currently an endangered species and rarely seen.

They have strong, powerful bodies, and the wings to carry them swiftly aloft.

Many think encountering one is a blessing, but they can be aggressive towards humans, so they should only be observed from a safe distance.

Egyptian Catfolk
Aegyptia cattus hominibus

This type of Catfolk is exclusive to
Egypt and only seemed to interact
with humans in Ancient Egypt. They
were often seen with or associated with
Egyptian Winged Cats and Egyptian
goddesses.

Most records of them are of female
cat-people, both winged and wingless.
It was confirmed that this species
still existed as late as 1938, but their
location and culture is kept private and
secret from humankind.

Cat Sidhe
Magicae cattus fae

Also know as a *Cat Sith*, this haunting creature has been spotted in the Scottish Highlands for hundreds of years. At first it was thought to be a ghost or specter of some sort, but it is now known to be a feline faerie species. Cat Sidhe are much larger than domestic cats, seeming closer in size to a large dog.

They most often appear as ginormous black cats with arched backs and bristled fur. A glowing white spot or spots can be seen on their chests. In full Fae form (very rare to see) this spot expands to a pattern of mystic swirls and possibly some sort of wings.

Legends say a Cat Sidhe should not be trusted and will steal the souls of those who have recently died before they can move on to the afterlife.

One can repel the creature from the bodies of the newly deceased by distracting it with riddles, music, or catnip. All nearby fires should be extinguished as well, for this ghostly feline is drawn to flame and warmth.

Winged Moon Cat
Volat luna cattus

Winged Moon Cats are beautiful, mysterious, and dangerous. They are only spotted in bright moonlight and even that is rare.

Those who encounter them will experience either great fortune or terrible bad luck depending on how the encounter goes.

Presenting the Moon Cat with flowers or baked goods can sway the interaction to the positive.

Attempting to catch a moon cat or treading upon its tail will have the worst results.

Anyone hissed at by a moon cat is said to be cursed and will suffer bad luck until either they or the moon cat dies.

Snow Dragopard
Panthera uncia draco

Native to Central and South Asia, the Snow Dragopard is an Asian Dragon and Slow Leopard hybrid first documented in the 18th century. As Snow Leopards have become scarcer due to destruction of their mountainous habitats, Snow Dragopards have followed suit and are now an extremely endangered species. Efforts to save the species are underway in Mongolia and China.

A carnivore, the Snow Dragopard preys on small mountain-dwelling mammals including sheep and goats, but never other felines. It is generally solitary, meeting with others of its kind only during mating season and to guard their eggs they have hatched. Lifespan is around fifty years, twice that of a Snow Leopard.

Star Tiger
Stella tigris

This extremely rare twelve foot celestial creature is only visible by the light of shooting stars. Because of this, much about the Star Tiger remains a mystery.

Some feel this species exists on another plane of being separate from ours. This plane is only visible and able to interact with ours in starlight. Others think there are only one or two Star Tigers in existence that are immortal and only visible when they choose to be.

Spotting one is said to be a beautiful and frightening experience. Those who have seen a Star Tiger may find themselves profoundly changed, becoming more aware of the universe and the connections between all living things than they were before.

Pegicornion
Pegasus+Unicorn+Lion

This unusual feline hybrid combines a lion with a pegasus and unicorn. Baby Pegicornions are extremely charming and charismatic. Adults are wise, noble, creatures. The properties of the horn of this creature are unknown as there are no records of anyone killing one. It is said that only faeries can ride them and that elder fae sometimes use them as mounts during the Wild Hunt.

Winged Saber-Tooth
Sparassodonta volans

A rare hybrid of the Saber-Tooth Cat and some sort of prehistoric winged creature, the Winged Saber-Tooth has been dated back as far as 42 million years ago. Several partial skeletons have been recovered.

What caused the winged form to evolve or the flying species involved is not known. A number of wizards have tried to magically resurrect this legendary feline, but so far all attempts have failed.

South African Catalope
Cattus bestia inlaqueata

This leopard-antelope hybrid is found solely in South Africa. The coat color of the creature varies greatly from pale yellow all the way to a golden orange. A few claim to have spotted a black variation of the species, but this could just be a tall-tale.

The Catalope has large antlers and spends much of its time in massive trees where it eats, sleeps, and stalks potential prey from above.

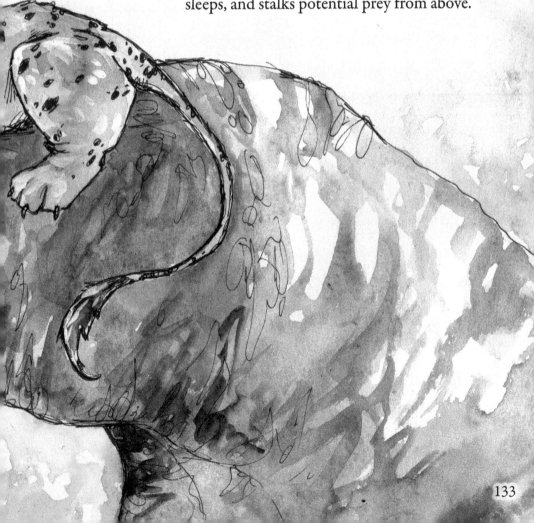

PLANT &
GARDEN

In this section you will meet monsters, dragons, and other creatures that are part plant, and/or are closely connected to plants, forests, and gardens.

Remember, even a harmless looking pretty flower may have nasty, razor-sharp teeth and be ready to bite off a finger, toe, or your entire head. Proceed with caution!

Monster Gardens

Monster plants and monster gardens have become more and more popular in the magic community the last ten years or so. They can protect a magicians' home or workshop, be a great showpiece (magic users are often trying to one-up each other), and even provide rare magical ingredients for spells or potions.

When the monster garden craze first began, a group of gardening witches from Northern England attempted to start a Monster Flower and Garden Show. After about half the witches and most of the spectators were eaten by the plants, it was decided the show should not be held in following years.

Monster gardens contain a variety of plants that range in both size and rarity. There is usually at least one extremely rare plant that serves as the centerpiece of the garden .

These types of gardens began in Europe where they featured many species of deadly flowers, vines with minds of their own, and even eye-ball plants to watch for intruders or pests.

Gradually magical folk in other climates began their own monster gardens too. These range from drier desert gardens with monster cacti and even sentient rocks to tropical gardens with monster palms, deadly jungle chompers, and spitting cobra plants.

Today magicians are also attempting beautiful and dangerous crossbreeds of plants such as the Man-Eating Snapper Rose. There is much debate as to if this is really neat... or just a really bad idea.

Prehistoric Daisy Flytrap
Bellis perennis droseraceae monstra

Prehistoric plant fibers magically recovered from fossils are the newest craze in monster-plant hybrids. The most affordable of these is the Prehistoric Daisy Flytrap which makes a wonderful small indoor or outdoor potted plant. The Daisy Flytrap is able to thump about to move its pot and will do so to chase down flies and any other pesky insects near it.

Daisy Chompers
Bellis perennis morsus duris

The Daisy chomper began as a common European Lawn
Daisy (*Bellis perennis*) that somehow mutated into a
chomper plant. Chomper plants are carnivorous monster
plants with one or more heads and, often, a large tangle of
roots they can use to ensnare victims. Daisy chompers rarely
grow over a few feet in height, but with multiple snapping
heads they should be considered highly dangerous.

Leaf Wyvern
Ligno frondoso planta draco

A dragon-plant creature, the Leaf Wyvern is under a foot in size and able to change colors in order to blend in with green or brown foliage. Fairly common in woodland areas and small forests throughout Europe, North America, and Canada. Only eats bugs and plants and is not considered dangerous to humans.

Monstrous Garden Hydra

Hortus planta hydrae

At three feet, this plant-creature may not seem all that intimidating, but its hydra DNA allows it to grow back multiple heads should you "deadhead" one. Each head has hundreds of tiny sharp teeth and craves raw meat. Must be fed on a regular schedule to keep it from consuming any nearby small animals or gardeners.

Agave Dragon
Agavoideae draco

Found in the arid regions of North America and the tropical regions of South America, the Agave Dragon is a plant-dragon hybrid with large, leafy scales. These scales are lined with sharp teeth-like barbs.

This species can grow up to six feet long. The females mate only once. They lay their eggs in a well-hidden cave, but the egg-laying process causes the female to die and the males must then guard the nest and baby Agave Dragons until they are large enough to fend for themselves. A high percentage of the eggs laid are female which helps to balance out their shorter lifespan.

Potted Chomper
Morsus mortiferum planta

Probably the best known of potted monster plants, Potted Chompers range in size from younger plants only a few inches high to adults growing up to eight feet tall. The growth is directly proportional to how much raw meat the plant is fed. Larger specimens can be very dangerous so only the most experienced or arrogant of monster gardeners attempt to grow their Chompers over two feet.

Agave Chomper Plant
Morsus mortiferum agavoideae

The Agave-Chomper monster plant is fairly rare and only found in the American Southwest, mainly in secret magical gardens, but there are a few that have sprouted in the desert as well. Appears to be a typical Agave plant until it grows a stalk that blooms with a number of large, deadly, carnivorous heads.

Tufted Mint Wyverns
Caespitosi mentam draco

Tiny garden plant-dragons, these Wyverns have bright colors and often come out to play and catch insects. This species is considered desirable in magical gardens both as a form of pest control and because they shed small mint-scented tufts every few days that are used in many potions. Requires special fae glow-lights to maintain a healthy population.

Calla Lily Drake

Zantedeschia aethiopica draco

Native to Africa, but can be found worldwide anywhere where Calla Lilies are grown or imported. Loves marshy areas where it can find a supply of the lilies it craves. Like the showy flowers they are drawn to, this dragon species like to show off for both dragons and humans. Kept as an ornamental pet and showpiece by medieval lords and ladies who could afford to import such exotic creatures.

Tree-Crowned Drake

Lignum coronam draco

Found in temperate deciduous forests worldwide. With bark-like scales and a tree growth upon their backs and/or heads this species is rarely noticed except by well trained and extremely patient dragon watchers.

Tree-Crowned Drakes are able to hold still for many hours at a time only to suddenly pounce on a small woodland mammal and snap it down in just a few bites. May grow as large as eight feet tall.

Tree-Crowned Wyrm

Lignum coronam serpentis draco

The Tree-Crowned Wyrm is much larger than the Tree-Crowned Drake, growing up to thirty feet in length. This Wyrm wraps itself around the trunks and branches of large trees which, combined with its branch-like growths, bark textured scales, and forest colors, make it an extremely well camouflaged and dangerous predator.

<u>Sakura Bark Wyrm</u>
Cerasus flores serpentis draco

A smaller Asian dragon, the Sakura Bark Wyrm is only a few feet in length. This species is named for the home it makes in the branches of Cherry Blossom trees. Found mainly in Japan and not considered dangerous to humans if it is left alone.

Garden Luck Drake
Hortus fortuna draco minor

A small, fuzzy luck dragon, around six inches long. Species can be identified by the butterfly-like wings and iridescent coloration. This dragon was once quite common in wildflower fields and gardens, but made rarer in the 1960s when it was discovered the wings of this creature, if dried and ground to a powder, were a powerful hallucinogen.

Manta Lung
Oxyopsis gracilis draco

Fossils of Manta Lungs have been found dating back 120 million years making it one of the earliest insect-dragon hybrid creatures.

Manta Lungs today are around 14 inches long, while the prehistoric variety grew up to three times that size.

This species prefers Neotropical climates and is thought to be related to *Oxyopsis gracilis* (the South American Green Mantis).

Manta Lungs are skilled at stalking their prey and have a diet mainly consisting of arthropods (insects, spiders etc).

Flora Conjuring Drake
Flos magi draco

This earth dragon is part of the *conjuring* class of dragons, something only recently discovered. Dragons in this grouping are able to use magic to conjure something, usually elemental based. This specific species can conjure small flowers and leaves which aid in its camouflage and evasion of predators.

Greater Earth Lung
Terra orientalium draco maior

A large dragon found in Japan, China, and Korea. Greater
Earth Lungs are only spotted by the most diligent of dragon
watchers willing to hike into the secluded mountain forests
where they dwell. Legends say they can grant those worthy
with elemental earth powers by gifting them with some sort of
bizarre leafy plant to ingest.

Red Butterfly Wyverns

There are two different red butterfly wyvern species that were, until recently, thought to be one. The first has a longer snout and yellow belly, and the second a pink belly and shorter snout. Both species attract butterflies, but the yellow-bellied variety prefers more tropical forests, while the pink-bellied variety likes European woodlands.

The relationship between these species and butterflies is still being studied. Both are herbivores, eating fruit and leafy plants.

Rock & Stone

In this section you will find earth creatures that are somehow related to rock or stone.

Some have bodies that resemble stone. Some are partly made of living rocks or gemstones. A few even create crystals and stones.

Others simply choose to make their homes near specific types of rocks or stones which creates an association between them.

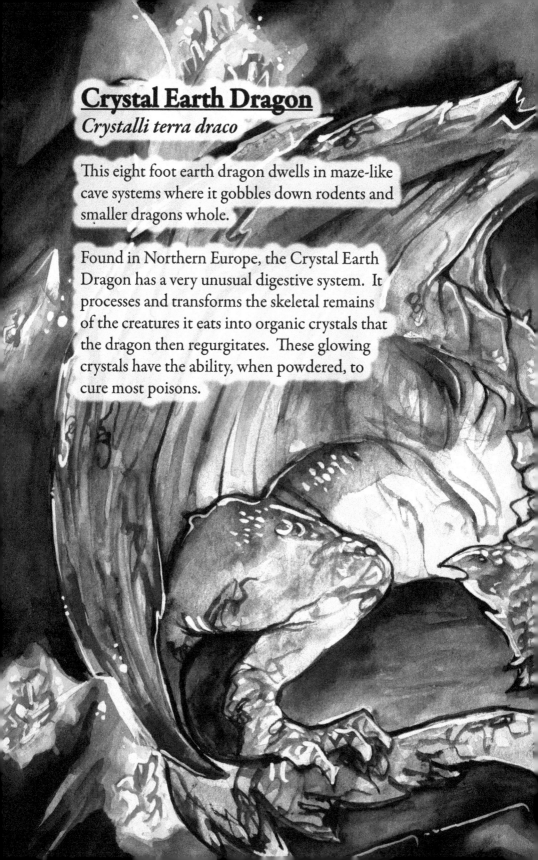

Crystal Earth Dragon
Crystalli terra draco

This eight foot earth dragon dwells in maze-like cave systems where it gobbles down rodents and smaller dragons whole.

Found in Northern Europe, the Crystal Earth Dragon has a very unusual digestive system. It processes and transforms the skeletal remains of the creatures it eats into organic crystals that the dragon then regurgitates. These glowing crystals have the ability, when powdered, to cure most poisons.

Ruby Rock Drake

Rubinus petram draco

This five inch red cave dragon can be found near large deposits of rubies in India, Cambodia, and Thailand.

Ruby Rock Drakes can be used to locate such deposits, but they are very fast moving and can breathe scalding blasts of fire as well, making them tricky to work with.

Amazonstone Coatl

Viridi lapis draco

The Amazonstone Coatl is both large (up to forty feet in length) and extremely rare. A feathered wyvern, it inhabits South America and is named for the blue-green Amazonite (aka Amazonstone) growths along its face and back.

Experts have determined that this dragon is a hybrid of earth and air species which explains the presence of both rock and feather anatomy. As far as is known this hybridization occurred naturally several thousand years ago.

It should be noted that Amazonstone deposits are rarely found in the amazon in spite of the stone being named for the area. There are theories that this is due to shed stones from this dragon species rather than deposits in the earth itself.

Moonstone Luck Lung
Luna lapis draco

This small two foot lung can be found in well-concealed rock dens near Moonstone deposits. Most recent reports of nests are from India and Sri Lanka.

The properties of this luck lung are very strange and still a bit of a mystery. They appear to be able to grant wishes, but only while holding large moonstones under the full moon. The size and success of the wishes granted relates to the size and purity of the moonstone used.

When the wish is made the moonstone and lung dragon are said to glow brightly for a few moments and then both vanish. It is not known if the wishes cause the dragon to perish or simply send it to a Moonstone deposit to recharge. Concerns about testing the wishing process without harming the test subjects have put a halt to further study, at least for the moment.

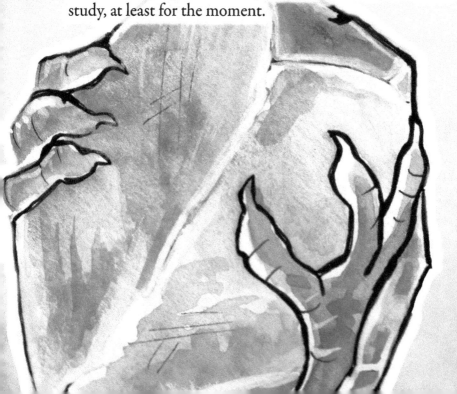

Sunstone Lung
Sol lapis draco

While similar in appearance to the Moonstone Lung, the Sunstone Lung is a little larger with adults reaching up to 3.5 feet. Sunstone Lungs can be found in Norway, Sweden, and occasionally North America.

This species is said to bring great strength to those who pay it tribute with gemstones of red, yellow, and orange hues. It is, of course, especially fond of the Sunstones it is named after and often chooses a rocky den near deposits of Sunstone or Quartz.

Those blessed by this dragon describe gaining a strength of heart, or character, rather than physical strength.

Amber Butterfly Drake
Papilio visio electri draco

This insectoid dragon species is about four inches tall and very skittish around humans and other creatures. A herbivore, the Amber Butterfly Drake eats mainly wildflowers, but babies have been observed chewing and teething on pinecones.

Originally thought to be amber in color, observation of baby specimens has shown otherwise. We now know the dragon itself has shimmering, slightly translucent scales without much color. The amber coloration occurs as the young dragons coat themselves in the sap from nearby pines. This sap hardens into an armor-like coating to help protect against predators.

Magma Dragoyle

Lava lapis draco

This smaller lava dragon-gargoyle hybrid is around three feet in length and fairly common near active volcanoes. Should the volcano become dormant the Magma Dragoyle will turn to stone and appear to be just an odd-shaped rock or crude carving. Exposure to volcanic gasses will bring the creature back to life. It is not known what the full lifespan of Magma Dragoyles is.

Lava Wyrm
Saxa liquefacta draco

One of the smaller lava dragon species, Lava Wyrms are usually under fifteen feet long when full grown.

Lava Wyrm eggs are left unattended once laid, but are so well camouflaged as to appear to be a pile of rocks to all but the most well trained observer.

The eggs are around a foot in diameter and are usually seen in groups of three to five. They remain totally dormant until a flow of lava heats them. Within a few moments the Lava Wyrm babies will break free of their shells and bathe in the hot lava (as shown here) until it cools. They will then seek out the surface and hunt as a group to find their first meal.

Lesser Lava Demon
Monstrum saxa liquefacta minor

This lesser variety of Lava Demon reaches full size around twenty feet in height. Lava Demons only make an appearance in pools of molten lava. They can be spotted during lava flows or by expeditions sent deep underground in search of rare earth creatures.

Lesser Lava Demons are often seen with dragons perched on their horns or arms, but the species of these dragons and their relationship to the demon has not been determined.

It is also worth noting that this creature was named due to its somewhat frighting appearance and large horns, but in all truth there is not anything evil or demonic about it.

Modern research shows that this is some form of earth giant or earth elemental creature. Unfortunately temperatures of over 1300 degrees (Fahrenheit) make it difficult to study or attempt communication with.

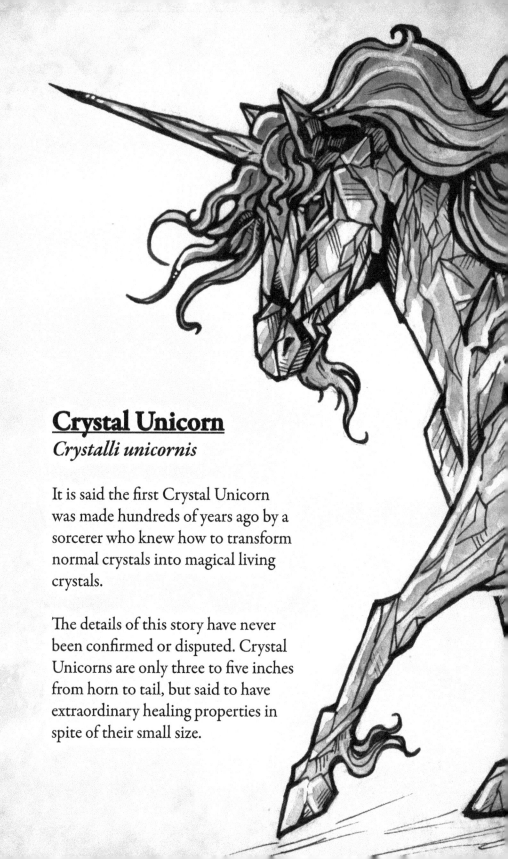

Crystal Unicorn

Crystalli unicornis

It is said the first Crystal Unicorn was made hundreds of years ago by a sorcerer who knew how to transform normal crystals into magical living crystals.

The details of this story have never been confirmed or disputed. Crystal Unicorns are only three to five inches from horn to tail, but said to have extraordinary healing properties in spite of their small size.

Amethyst Troll
Amethystus troglodytarum

A Lesser known troll species, the fifteen foot tall Amethyst Troll is actually part living amethyst itself. The hard rocky growths keep developing and sometimes breaking off as long as the troll is alive.

This species is cave-dwelling and found mainly in Brazil. They will eat humans if presented with the opportunity, so anyone looking to observe this creature should do so undetected if they want to live.

WATER
FOLK

Mysterious water creatures ranging from
the depths of the ocean to those going
unnoticed in small rural ponds have been
placed in this section.

There are dragons, merfolk, and even some
stranger sea people to be found within!

Rainbow Ruins Serpent

Eritque arcus aquaum antiquorum draco

A sea-dwelling water dragon, this beautiful rainbow species is only reported around underwater ruins and thus is said to be somehow related to the lost city of Atlantis. As with most things tied to Atlantis there is no hard evidence to prove a connection.

Rainbow Ruins Serpents range in size from twenty-five to sixty feet long. Shed scales turn pale white and lose all but a slight rainbow sheen immediately, making it apparent that something about the living dragon itself causes the bright colors to appear.

Lesser Pond Serpent
Stagno minor draco

Between ten and fourteen inches in length, this species is found only in smaller freshwater bodies like ponds and small lakes. Lesser Pond Serpents are VERY timid. When startled they will quickly dive below the surface and hide among shoreline vegetation. Once hidden they are extremely hard to locate. Feeds on insects, small fish, and frogs.

Coral Reef Wyvern

Alcyoneum scopulum draco minor

Around forty inches, this sea wyvern is a small dragon that dwells around colorful coral in order to camouflage itself. It is able to shift the colors of its coral-like horns and mane to better blend in. This is used both to hide from predators and to hunt small fish which it will suddenly snap up as they pass.

Seaside Serpent
Litus aquae draco

This water dragon chooses to frequent seaside areas ranging from North America to Australia. Around 15 feet long the Seaside Serpent is often spotted by tourists at the beach, only to be gone a moment later. Why the species chooses to tease humans in such a way is a mystery.

Ocean Conjurer Drake
Oceani magi draco

Conjurer Dragons are a class of dragon species able to use magic to bring forth or create something that wasn't there before. The Ocean Conjurer Drake is able to create water currents, heat, air pockets, and even algae. These talents seem to be mainly used to balance the underwater environment for about five or six miles around where the drake makes its den.

Blue-Scaled Water Drake
Caerulea scalis aqua draco

A South American freshwater dragon species, the Blue-Scaled Water Drake is carnivorous and feeds on smaller freshwater fish, snakes, dragons, and whatever else it can find. The scales of the male dragon become brighter blue and may even turn other colors during mating season to attract a mate. The scales and teeth of the species are much sought after ingredients for spells involving changing the color of ones eyes or hair permanently.

Finnish Fisher Drake

Fennica piscantur draco

This dragon species can be found in parts of Canada, but is best known in Finland. One of the most proficient fishing dragons alive today, the Finnish Fisher Drake catches large freshwater fish with ease. It seems to favor Pike the most, when they can be found.

Look for them near cold, clear, rocky waters, but it is advised to only watch from a distance as they are strong both on land and underwater and have very powerful jaws.

Shell Warrior Merfolk
Testa bellator syreni

Shell Warrior Merfolk are only around eight to ten inches when full grown. In spite of their small size they are fierce warriors capable of taking down much larger water dragons, fish, and even sharks. A group of these merfolk can capsize small human watercraft and even kill humans if they feel threatened by them.

Shell Warriors craft their armor and weapons from the hardest of seashell shards and coral.

This species rides large *Frilled Seahorse Dragons* which are trained, from birth, to be brave and loyal. A dragon and merfolk are usually paired for life. Most Shell Warriors value the life of their dragon over their own and will do anything to protect it.

Lost Coral Merfolk

Absentis alcyoneum syreni

This merfolk species was once friendly and social with humans, but humankind abused this privilege.

Historical records tell of humans who lured the most beautiful Coral Merfolk to the surface with promises of treasure and then captured them for use in sideshows. They also hunted the Sea Dragicorns raised by the Coral Merfolk and stole valuable magical artifacts from Coral Merfolk villages.

This caused these merfolk to hide themselves away from humans permanently. It is thought that they still have huge coral cities, but only in massive secret underwater caverns. The entrances to these are cleverly disguised to keep anyone who would find them away.

Sea Dragicorn
Draco unicornis maris

A seahorse-dragon-unicorn hybrid, this creature is around seven feet in length. This species was (and may still be) bred by the Lost Coral Merfolk who use them for transportation. Around the early 1800s it was discovered that powdered Sea Dragicorn horn could be used in a potion giving the magician the ability to breathe underwater permanently. For this reason the species was hunted almost to extinction. Those that remain have been carefully hidden away by the Lost Coral Merfolk. Scale colors vary and can include purple, pink, and blue.

Orca Folk
Orcinus orca femina

A little-known sea-folk species, Orca Folk are humanoid-whale
creatures. They are larger than humans, ranging from twelve
to fifteen feet from head to tail. Like Orca Whales, they have
a pack based society where they live, and hunt, in groups of up
to ten. They will hunt fish, sharks, and even rays. They tend to
avoid humans, perhaps because they are kin to whale species that
humans have hunted.

Fishfolk
Pisces homo

Known as the "reverse mermaid" from 1930s sideshows,
Fishfolk are a human-fish hybrid, but much more fish than
human. They are around three and a half feet tall and often
frighten humans who spot them with their large glassy
eyes. In reality Fishfolk are herbivores who mainly feed on
seaweed and are very gentle.

Fishkie

Nympharum pisces

This tiny four inch fresh water creature is a hybrid of fish and pixie. They can be found in secluded woodland ponds where they splash and frolic with dragonflies and tease hungry toads.

Pearl Merfolk

Syreni bacca

Pearl Merfolk from the South China Sea have a unique society structured around the growth and trade of pearls that they farm. They trade with human fishermen, other merfolk species, and assorted other water creatures.

The pearls this merfolk species grows in their oyster farms seem to glow slightly and bring good fortune to those who wear them. They are also used by magicians to add extra power to their water elemental spells.

Mercaelia Folk
Femina piscis lolligo

This mysterious underwater creature is a hybrid of Cecaelia (squid people) and Merfolk (fish people) and thus has both fins and tentacles.

Only a handful of such hybrids have ever been reported. They are almost always seen with sea serpents, but it is not clear how many of the species exist or what their bond with water dragons may be.

Deep-Sea Merfolk

Abyssi aequor syreni

Found in the deepest parts of the ocean, this species of merfolk is able to survive in much harsher conditions than merfolk found closer to the surface. They are adept at hunting other deep-sea creatures with little or no light and their bodies can withstand much higher pressure and extremely cold water temperatures.

Deep-Sea Merfolk do not venture into the upper parts of the ocean and were only recently discovered deep in the Pacific Ocean. Those studying them doubt they could survive the higher oxygen concentration in the water closer to the surface which keeps them below 3500 feet.

There are rumors that they have deep-sea kingdoms with elaborate buildings and great monuments. But those sent to find them have either gone mad or never returned at all.

DOMESTICATED CRITTERS

These creatures have worked their way into our lives in our cities, towns, and homes. Many of these species have been living with us for hundreds of years mostly unnoticed, while others are fairly new arrivals.

Some choose to bond with and aid humans as helpers, companions and pets. Others may steal from us or play tricks on us for their own pleasure.

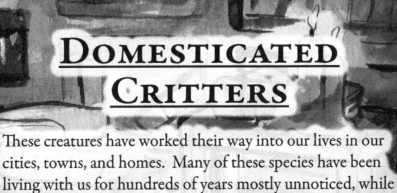

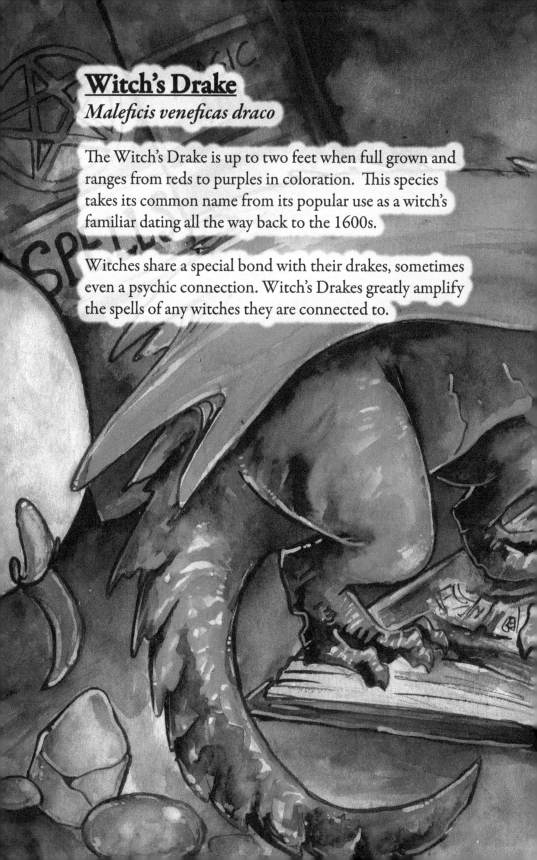

Witch's Drake
Maleficis veneficas draco

The Witch's Drake is up to two feet when full grown and ranges from reds to purples in coloration. This species takes its common name from its popular use as a witch's familiar dating all the way back to the 1600s.

Witches share a special bond with their drakes, sometimes even a psychic connection. Witch's Drakes greatly amplify the spells of any witches they are connected to.

Forge Drake
Fornacem ferrarii draco

Forge or Smithy Drakes are a species of red fire dragon trained to assist in forges throughout the 19th century. These mid-sized western dragons were carefully tamed and trained from hatching until they grew too big for convenience in the respective smithy or forge.

Their tasks included starting the forge fire and keeping it burning at consistent high temperatures, scaring off or killing any rodents, and guarding the valuable metals and tools from would-be thieves.

Forge Drake domestication, of course, included training them to keep the fire contained within the hearth and not catch any humans on fire. This *mostly* worked.

Lesser Moss Drake
Musci draco minor

A smaller Moss Dragon, this gentle forest creature loves other animals and often bonds with them. This species has had some successes as a domestic pet, but only in very calm and safe environments.

In such cases it has been shown that the company of another pet such as a ferret, kitten, puppy, or rat will make the Lesser Moss Drake much happier.

This species is a herbivore and can have a sensitive stomach.

Cake-Guzzler
Crustulam comedenti draco

Baby Cake-Guzzlers are so adorable they often get away with pillaging cakes from pantries and bakeries. But, left unchecked, this dragon species will eat every cake in sight and grow larger at an extremely rapid pace.

One test specimen, when allowed to eat cakes constantly, grew so quickly that within a week it was able to eat the entire research facility.

The rapid growth and growing appetite only seems to occur if the species is fed cake. They are deemed quite safe if kept on a strict healthy diet of fruit and vegetables.

Art Drakes

Art Drakes are a group of small, colorful, dragon species trained to paint in the late 1970s. This fad was quite popular among keepers of rare magical creatures at the time. The messy psychedelic paintings of Art Drakes sold for hundreds of thousands of dollars.

In the mid 1980s environmentalist dragon watchers protested that the paint fumes were shortening the lives of the dragons and Art Drakes quickly went out of style.

Red-Scaled Pencil Snatcher
Rubrum pencillorum furem draco

A plague to schools and universities, this quick dragon loves to snatch up pencils and sneak them away to a hidden lair. These pencil-troves are usually somewhere in the walls of the school.

The Red-Scaled Pencil Snatcher eats the lead found in the pencils and nests on a springy bed of leftover erasers.

Most common in older buildings, particularly prep schools and academies in the United Kingdom.

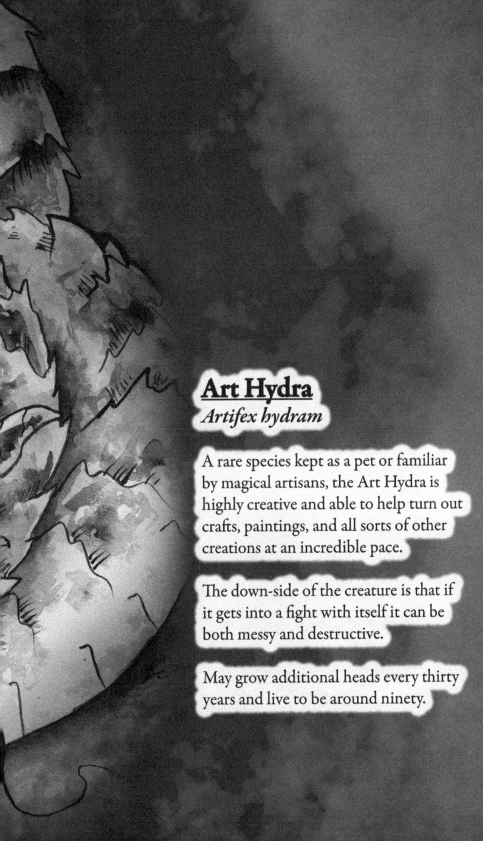

Art Hydra
Artifex hydram

A rare species kept as a pet or familiar by magical artisans, the Art Hydra is highly creative and able to help turn out crafts, paintings, and all sorts of other creations at an incredible pace.

The down-side of the creature is that if it gets into a fight with itself it can be both messy and destructive.

May grow additional heads every thirty years and live to be around ninety.

The Purple Snatcher
Purpura furem draco

A small purple dragon around eight pounds when full-grown. Their adorable appearance as babies often causes children to bring them home to keep as hidden pets.

Unfortunately, the Purple Snatcher has an irrepressible urge to snatch things that we are using. This is akin to a kitten trying to get a toy from a human, but much faster and they never outgrow it.

Those living with purple snatchers often spend hours searching for pencils, pens, toothbrushes, egg sandwiches and other weird things the dragon has snatched impulsively.

Snack Snatcher

Omnia quaerunt furem draco

Colorful and stealthy, this species of dragon loves human snacks, particularly crackers and chips of any kind. At five inches, this drake isn't as noticeable as one would expect. They will slip silently, sometimes in groups of three or four, into a bag of chips and softly crunch them all up, leaving only crumbs and a few tiny blue-green scales behind.

Holly Drake
Aquifoliaceae draco minor

This gentle, playful drake is active mainly in the winter where it is drawn to all species of holly plant. This urge to attack and chew the leaves and berries of holly plants is uncontrollable.

Since Holly berries and leaves are, at best, sickening to most other species, it is extremely strange that this dragon has no adverse reactions.

Recently it has been put forward that the dragon may actually experience a euphoric high from holly similar to how many felines react to catnip.

For some, this dragon is considered a symbol of the winter holidays as it is often seen rolling in the snow with holly around that time of year.

Axolotl Drake

Ambystoma mexicanum draco

This hybrid of dragon and axolotl was first discovered in freshwater lakes in Mexico. It is incredibly rare and thus is considered highly valuable as an exotic magical pet.

A carnivorous dragon species, the Axolotl Drake must be fed live worms or fish.

This creature can regrow lost limbs and even lost wings in a few weeks, but unlike hydra dragon species they cannot regrow their head and will die if it is cut off. While a normal Axolotl can only grow back a given limb five times, the drake hybrid does not seem to have this limitation.

The limbs of the Axolotl Drake are sometimes used for spells, but repeated removal of all the limbs will tax the healing powers of the creature too much and it will die. This is thought to be one reason they are so rare today. Lifespan is around twenty to twenty five years when allowed to live normally.

Bearded Dragon Drake

Pogona vitticeps draco

This species was engineered by a group of magical exotic pet traders in the early 1990s with a specific goal of creating a desirable domesticated lizard-dragon hybrid.

They succeeded and today the Bearded Dragon Drake is one of the most common starter pets for young wizards and witches. The shed scales of this dragon can be used for many low-level spells and potions including a water to wine spell which often gets younger magicians into trouble.

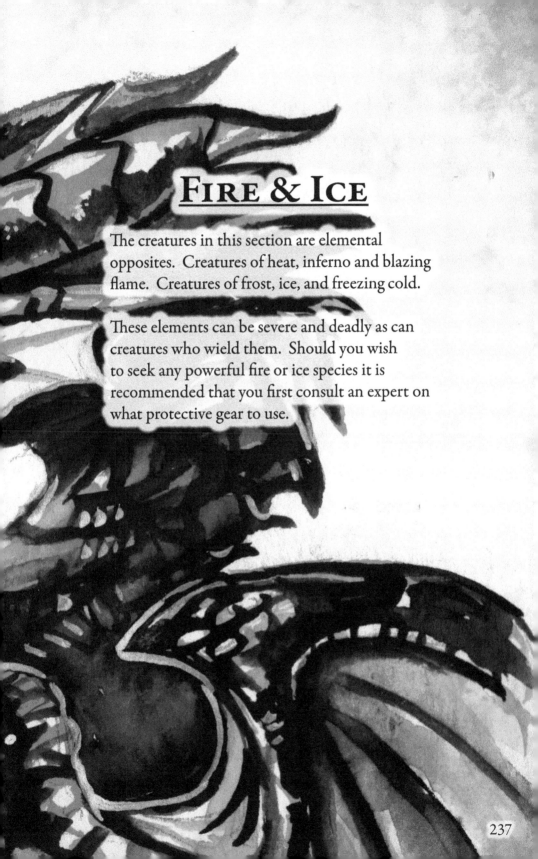

FIRE & ICE

The creatures in this section are elemental opposites. Creatures of heat, inferno and blazing flame. Creatures of frost, ice, and freezing cold.

These elements can be severe and deadly as can creatures who wield them. Should you wish to seek any powerful fire or ice species it is recommended that you first consult an expert on what protective gear to use.

Elder Frost Wyvern
Antiquorum gelu draco

These are creatures of legend, but rarely seen today. Mighty fifty foot dragons with dangerously cold breath that can freeze entire fields of crops in one swoop, even if the weather was quite pleasantly warm moments before.

Last reported frost that was attributed to an Elder Frost Wyvern was in the early 1900s. They are still thought to exist, but be in a deep hibernation at this time.

Window Frost Drake
Fenestram gelu draco

This frost dragon is only around three inches tall, but able to coat massive areas in frost with each breath. For some reason it is drawn to "frosting" smooth surfaces. In the wild this includes ponds, lakes, and smooth rocks. In areas settled by humans this includes the windows of homes and cars. They are swift and stubborn too. When humans scrape away their frost, they will swoop in and quickly re-coat the surface again.

Butterfly Snow Wyvern

Papilio draco nix

The Butterfly Snow Wyvern, named for it's delicate butterfly-like wings, is only active in temperatures below 20 degrees (Fahrenheit). The ice-like reflective scales of this twenty-two inch creature make it hard to spot in snow and ice. This species will breathe a stream of snow into the eyes of any predators or attackers it feels threatened by. While not that harmful, it causes enough impaired vision for the little dragon to escape.

Northern Blizzard Wyvern
Septemtrionis nix tempestas draco

This twenty foot creature is rarely spotted as it is only active during the worst of blizzards. Sightings have mainly been in Canada and occasionally the northern United States.

There is much debate among both dragon and storm watchers as to if the Blizzard Wyvern follows the blizzards or somehow causes them.

Many who have tried to study the species have perished, frozen to death by either the storm or the icy breath of the Blizzard Wyvern.

Snow Behemoth

Colossus nix bestia draconis

A hulking titan of the arctic, the Snow Behemoth is a massive sixty foot dragon species. Snow Behemoths are only found in glacier caves and mostly go unnoticed. This is due to their 150 year hibernation cycle.

While hibernating they are covered in snow and ice, appearing to simply be part of the cave itself. A few experienced dragon watchers know the locations of several such creatures in hibernation, but are not comfortable disclosing the information for publication should it be exploited for nefarious purposes.

Iridescent Spark Drake
Minima scintilla draco

A tiny half-inch tall wingless drake with a thick tail and iridescent glowing scales. Lives in little rocky hollows, miniature caves, and tunnels in the Southwestern United States. Can be helpful in starting campfires with its tiny sparks.

Incandescent Flame Wyvern
Draco flamma candens

A sixty-to-eighty foot fire dragon spotted only at the exact moment of sunset. There are a large number of unproven theories about the creature including that it is a cross-dimensional dragon, that its scales have some special properties making it invisible except in very specific lighting, that it is the visual manifestation of some magical event, and so on. There are, of course, those who insist it doesn't exist at all and that it is a hallucination cause by staring into the sun.

Miniature Flame Wyvern
Incendit minima draco

This tiny dragon is no more than an inch in size, often even smaller. They start fires and are drawn to fires already burning, but are usually mistaken for flames or sparks. Can cause serious burns if handled without proper protection. One should not startle a Miniature Flame Wyvern as it can dart about in panic and quickly start a large and deadly fire.

Ember Lung

Orientales ignem prunae draco

This small six inch Japanese lung dragon loves to crawl into
the warm embers of dying fires and fall asleep. Later, if startled
awake, it scatters the remains of the fire everywhere which
leads to a chaotic mess. This species is not fire-breathing and is
harmless aside from leaving sooty footprints everywhere.

Purple Spiral Wyvern
Purpura spiralem caelo draco

With pronounced ridges, spikes, and distinctive spiral patterns this red fire dragon has a name that causes much confusion in the dragon watching community.

It was discovered one night in the mountains of Germany by a small group of dragon watchers. Agitated, the dragon attacked breathing fire at the party who quickly retreated, but not before snapping a few flash-photos.

The fire this wyvern species breathes is purple in color and, in the darkness, it reflected off the scales of the dragon making it appear purple too. The dragon was later discovered to actually be red, but by then the name had stuck and has been used ever since.

Ancient & Celestial

The creatures placed here are often associated with the sun, stars, shadows, or moon.

They can be great warriors, shadowy creatures, or mythic beasts. Many have appeared in myths and legends, been worshiped as gods, or feared as monsters.

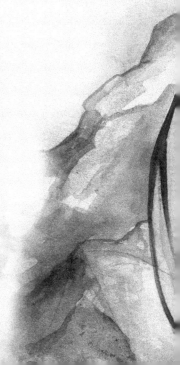

Kitsune
Femina vulpes mutatio

This creature is well-known throughout Asia, particularly in Japan. A shape-shifter, the Kitsune can take the form of a human, fox, or any combination of the two.

The human form is almost always a female, often in fairly elaborate and beautiful clothing. One should be extremely careful when dealing with a Kitsune, as with all fox and wolf creatures, for trickery is in their nature.

Shadow Kitsune
Femina vulpes mutatio umbra

The Shadow Kitsune is only active at night, slipping silently through the shadows. She may appear as a temptress who will steal or trick those who fall for her beauty. This species is sometimes employed as spies both by humans and faeries.

Kitsune Tails

The more tails a Kitsune has the older, more intelligent, more cunning, and more powerful it is. Some species grow an additional tail every fifty years, while others only grow them after they have aged past a hundred. Most of the encounters from the last hundred years have been with Kitsune with five or fewer tails.

Kitsune with nine tails are said to be so powerful that they were considered gods by those who met them. They were hundreds, perhaps thousands, of years old and no human could ever outwit them. Some say these God Kitsune no longer have time to bother with humans, while others say they have become so wise that there are many of them among us, using their cunning and shape-shifting to appear human.

Light Kitsune
Femina vulpes mutatio levi

Most often encountered in daylight hours, this creature is considered the opposite and balance of the Shadow Kitsune. While she may still be a trickster, she will use her tricks on those who would harm others, often helping women to escape dangerous situations.

Shadow Drakes

Opertam draco (rubrum & viridi)

Shadow dragons are so named because they have an aversion to bright light. Shadow dragon species are the only dragons known to breathe black flame. The properties of this flame are very strange. Anything touched by it becomes charred and turns to ash, but it does not spread like normal fire and, if anything, resembles chaos magic more than flame.

Those burned by Shadow Dragons often lose their minds. The species is greatly feared by any who grew up with tales of the madness they can cause.

Red Shadow Drakes are smaller, around a foot in size, and more common. Green Shadow Drakes can be up to twelve feet in height and are less common. Found in North America, South America, and occasionally in Europe.

Celestial Unicorn
Caeleste unicornis

This creature was originally thought to be two rare species: the Solar and Lunar Unicorn. About ten years ago it was discovered it is actually one species that shifts between the two forms at the moment of sunrise and sunset. Only spotted from a distance on high cliff tops and said to be one of the most beautiful creatures in the world.

Elder Dragicorn

Antiquis unicornis draco

The oldest and largest of dragon-unicorn hybrids, only one living Elder Dragicorn is known of today and his location is a closely guarded secret known only to the highest members of the elementalist societies.

Stories say those who encounter an Elder Dragicorn learn the deepest truths about themselves. Those with a good heart will become more confident and powerful and those with bad intentions will wither and shrink in upon themselves.

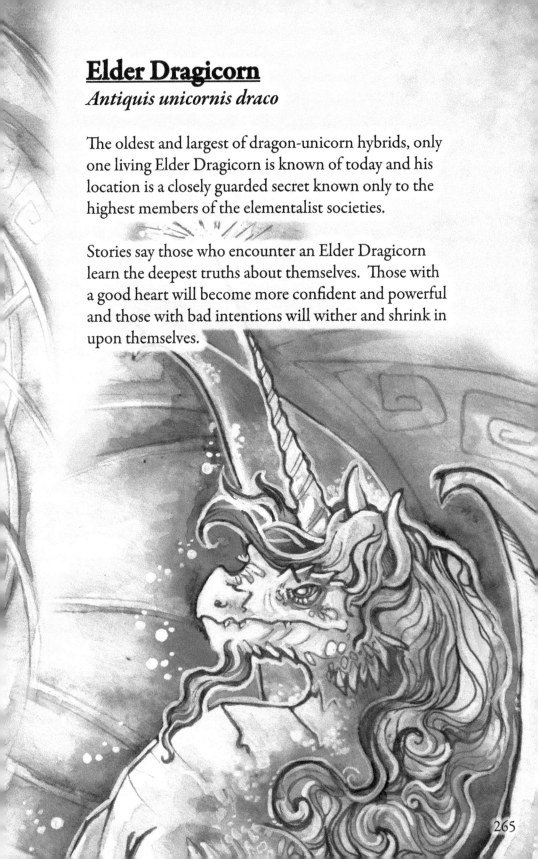

Solar Wyrm
Solaris serpens draco

The Solar Wyrm is often compared with the Lunar Wyrm as both like to bathe lazily in their respective elements. The species themselves are quite different, with Solar Wyrms sticking to rocky warmer climates, especially near geothermic activity. When observing this dragon use great care as it may appear to be dozing in the sun, only to snap you up for a snack so quickly you won't have time to react.

Lunar Wyrm
Lunaris serpens draco

Can be spotted in rocky areas moon bathing on brightly lit nights. Most common in China and Thailand. Size ranges from two to twelve feet and they appear larger on nights when the moon is full. The scales of the Lunar Wyrm will retain moonlight and glow for up to 48 hours after exposure which can be useful for spells requiring moonlight should they need to be performed during the day or indoors.

FEATHERED FRIENDS

Here you can find an assortment of feathered creatures from Griffins to Phoenixes and, of course, some feathered dragons too!

Some of these species are well known and others are only recently discovered. In many cases their shed feathers may even hold power, so please handle any strange feathers you find with caution!

Chinese Mountain Phoenix
Orientalium montem ignis avem

This species of phoenix is native to the mountainous forests of China. A few were introduced into the United Kingdom and North America when they were gifted as exotic pets to dignitaries or companions to sorcerers, but it is still very rare to spot one outside China.

One of the most unusual phoenix species, this colorful variety is fairly small with adults reaching full size at around 50 inches, including tail feathers.

Diet consists of berries, seeds, and small beetles. Like most phoenix species, this one has a cycle of regeneration that occurs when they reach around 60 years of age or are near death.

After a fiery death flare the phoenix is reborn in egg form to grow and live again. This species seems to retain knowledge between incarnations. Their total lifespan or number of regenerations is unknown.

Frogmouth Phoenix
Podargus strigoides ignis

A strange hybrid of Phoenix and Frogmouth birds, this creature can be differentiated from the typical phoenix by the short, squat body and wider mouth. A nocturnal species, the Frogmouth Phoenix can be up to two feet from crest to tail and has only been spotted in New Guinea. A carnivore, it will feed on anything from worms and snakes to small rodents and even dragons! The flaming aura shown here is only visible when the creature is agitated, excited, or has just been reborn.

Cheery Tufted Wyvern
Beatum parva draco

This small wyvern is only six to eight inches long when full grown. It was dubbed with the "Cheery" name as it always looks like it is smiling. This is one of the few species with webbed wings AND feathers. The feathers can be found as a head crest and as smaller tufts along the spine and edge of the wings. Lives in warm tropical caves where it feeds on insects and fruit. Can be lured out with mango or peach juice placed near the cave entrance.

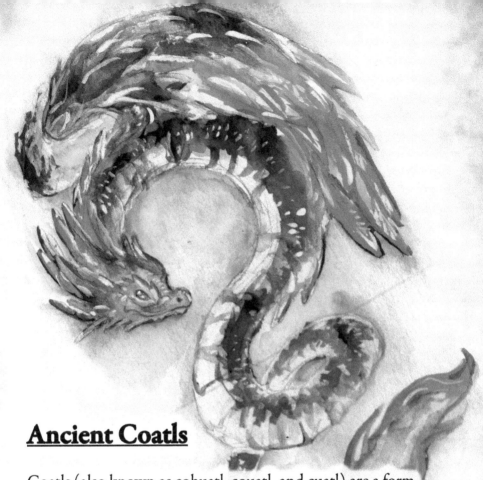

Ancient Coatls

Coatls (also known as cohuatl, couatl, and cuatl) are a form of feather winged serpent-dragon that have been around since prehistoric times. They are most common in Tropical and Neotropical locations. In ancient times they were revered by many cultures. One famous example was a shape-shifting form of Coatl (probably extinct today) that was known as the Aztec god Quetzalcoatl.

Another feathered serpent god, Kukulkan, was worshiped by the Maya. There are signs of feathered serpents and dragons going even farther back to the Olmec people, but no one has been able to verify if the creatures in their paintings are specific Coatl species, some sort of feathered wyrm without flight, or some other creature entirely.

Peacock Draconis

Pavo draco

This five foot colorful dragon is named after the male peafowl (peacock) due to a resemblance in color and the feather crest topping the dragon's head.

The Peacock Draconis was once kept in the gardens of emperors and kings, but it has dwindled in numbers over the last hundred years and is rarely found today.

The iridescent feathers of this avian dragon are said to make those who wear them appear more beautiful and can also be used in beautification spells.

<u>Tropical Dragoyle</u>
Bestia lapis tropicae draconis

A dragon-gargoyle hybrid, this species is around two feet long and nests high in rocky cliff faces. When active, it is brightly colored in variations of blue and green. Often goes dormant for months at a time where it appears to simply be another rocky bump on the cliff. Only found in the Republic of Seychelles. Known to startle awake with suddenly loud shrieks and scare vacationers climbing or bouldering in the area.

Lesser Butterfly Coatl

Papilio parva draco

This Coatl species was associated with butterflies back in the 1400s as it was often seen frolicking with large swarms of them. Further observation showed that this four foot air dragon feeds on the butterflies and is actually hunting them not engaging in a form of play.

Like the butterflies it consumes, the lifespan of the Lesser Butterfly Coatl is not very long, ranging from five to ten weeks. Upon death the creature, feathers and all, decays much more rapidly than one would expect and is only a pile of dust after a day or two.

Puffin Drake
Fratercula arctica draco

The Puffin Drake is a hybrid combining some form of prehistoric avian dragon with the Atlantic Puffin (*fratercula arctica*). It is unknown if this hybrid occurred naturally or as the result of an undocumented magical experiment.

Puffin Drakes have become more common recently, but reports of sightings can be traced back at least three hundred years. They are usually found in Norway, Iceland, and the Faroe Islands.

A proficient swimmer, the two foot tall Puffin Drake is also able to fly high enough to nest in seaside cliffs where it tries to hide itself from humans and other dragon species that may hunt for its eggs.

Golden Griffin
Aureum gryphem

This well-known creature appears in the art of many cultures including Ancient Egypt and Ancient Greece. It has also graced a number of flags and shields in coats of arms. This is the griffin species medieval knights most often battled.

Golden Griffins, if raised from the egg, can be tamed and ridden with relative ease. In the 1700s scouts and messengers often preferred this species of griffin over riding a similar-sized dragon or other flying creature. Today the art of Griffin taming and riding is much less common.

Jaybird Griffin
Also called the Blue Tufted Griffin

Only found in Canada and the North-East parts of North America, this creature is often mistaken for a large Blue Jay bird. Those who observe closely will spot feline hindquarters and a tail that set it apart from the bird species. Eats nuts, seeds, insects, worms, snails, and the occasional tiny mouse. Can be bold when hungry, even raiding bird feeders.

Nests can be found in the branches of tall pines, oaks, and fir trees. Jaybird Griffins may also make dens in the trunks of such trees to store away food for later. Can be aggressive in defense of a nest or den.

Griffin Owl

Nicknamed the "Growl"

Found in North America and some parts of Canada, the Griffin Owl or "Growl" is around 30 inches tall with a wingspan around five feet. A nocturnal hunter, this creature will eat mammals such as rabbits and mice, as well as small dragons when it can catch them.

<u>Grificorn</u>
Unicornis gryphem

The exact origin of this unicorn-griffin hybrid isn't known, but most theories say it was either genetically or magically engineered into being as there doesn't seem to be any natural cross-breeding of the species. Grificorns are small, only twenty inches when full grown, and contain massive amounts of magical power which seems to be related to the sun and solar cycles.

<u>Faeire Griffin</u>

Nymphalem naturae gryphem

A small two-to-three foot species, Faerie Griffins are a newer discovery. They have pastel colors, extremely sharp beaks, and strange striped feathers. A few have claimed these feathers have some sort of magical power, but the details are not clear at this time. The author has requested any new information be sent her way for inclusion in future books. Diet of the creatures includes berries, nuts, and most rodent species.

Resplendent Neotropical Griffin

Resplendens tropicae grypus

A smaller griffin species, this one is just a few feet in length.
Found only in Neotropical forests and humid highland areas.
The Neotropical Griffin is frugivorous (eating almost only
fruit), though baby Neotropical Griffins may be fed small frogs
or lizards as they are more nutritious and aid with growth.

The feathers of this griffin are iridescent and appear to change
color in sun or moonlight. They can range from green to yellow
to blue, with splashes of red or purple.

This species was thought to be some type of god by ancient
people including the Aztec and Maya. Some where even
the companions of great warriors. Those who wore the shed
feathers of these creatures were said to be fortunate and brave.

Wise Ravens
Corvus corax prudens

While all raven species are highly intelligent, these ravens are even more so. They can speak. They can build. They can even do minor magics.

Wise Ravens live many hundreds of years. In ancient times it was said that a pair of these ravens gathered information for the Norse god Odin.

While Wise Ravens are rarer today, they are still much sought after by witches and wizards as they are excellent advisors and can often find out things that no one else can.

293

Dear Reader,

And so...we have reached the end of this book.
I hope you have enjoyed all the weird creatures
and crazy critters contained within these pages!

Remember to look harder at things you spot out
of the corner of your eye, check for creatures
who may be stealing your loose change or snacks,
and hang on to every bit of magic you can find.

WANT MORE?

CHECK OUT ALL THE OTHER BOOKS
IN THE SERIES AT RAREDRAGONS.COM!

Index

About the Author

Jessica Cathryn Feinberg is a driven, quirky, creative gal who resides in Tucson, Arizona with a house full of books, cats, faeries, and other strange creatures.

Jessica has been fascinated by faeries and dragons since she was very young and has dedicated her life to writing, drawing, painting, and following in the footsteps of mysterious creatures. She is best known for her dragon, clockwork, and wildlife artwork as well as her field guides to rare creatures.

For more information please visit RareDragons.com